W9-CNV-006

# A Look at SNAKES

Written by Jerald Halpern

STECK-VAUGHN
ELEMENTARY · SECONDARY · ADULT · LIBRARY

A Harcourt Classroom Education Company

www.steck-vaughn.com

# Contents

# What Are Snakes?

    Snakes are found all over the world.
They can live in many different **habitats**.
They live mainly in warm places. They
do not live in very cold areas or high in
the mountains.

Most snakes live in the grass, on rocks, or in water. Some snakes live underground. Others even live in trees. Sea snakes live only in the ocean. They never go on land.

Snakes, crocodiles, turtles, and lizards are in the same animal family. They have dry skin that is covered with **scales**. They warm and cool their bodies by lying in the sun or the shade. They are called **reptiles**.

# What Do Snakes Look Like?

Snakes come in many different sizes. Some are small and thin. Others are large and thick. One of the very smallest snakes is the thread snake. It is about as long as an adult's foot and as thin as a piece of spaghetti.

The largest snake is the anaconda. It can grow to be thirty feet long. That is about as long as a school bus! Anacondas can be as big around as a large tree. They can weigh as much as 400 pounds. A baby elephant can weigh that much, too.

Snakes can be very colorful, with bright bands or patterns. They can also be a solid color, such as brown or gray. Their colors help them blend in with the things around them.

The skin of a snake is made up of many scales. These scales are very dry and shaped like fingernails. Sometimes the scales get thin and worn from the snake moving. When this happens, the snake replaces the skin with a new one. This is called **molting**.

Snakes move by sliding on their bellies. They are one of the slowest moving animals. Their bodies can bend very easily. They can **coil** themselves into a ball or stretch out straight.

Everything looks blurry to snakes because they cannot see well. They have no eyelids, so their eyes are open all the time. All snakes have forked tongues. They smell what is around them by flicking their tongues in and out.

# How Do Snakes Protect Themselves?

Snakes have many enemies, so they have to **protect** themselves. Some have the same colors on their bodies as the things around them. This **camouflage** helps hide snakes from their enemies.

Many snakes try to scare their
enemies away by making noises. Some
hiss loudly. Others shake their tail very
quickly. Rattlesnakes have a rattle on
the end of their tail. When they shake
it, a rattling sound can be heard.

Some snakes can change the shape of their bodies to protect themselves. Cobras coil up into a circle and make their necks grow wide. Then they **strike** forward and try to bite their enemy.

Snakes can use their poison, called
**venom**, to hurt or even kill enemies.
They bite with their poisonous **fangs**.
The king cobra is the largest poisonous
snake in the world. It has been known
to bite people.

Many snakes that are not poisonous act as if they are. King snakes and rat snakes rattle their tails to make a sound like a rattlesnake. Some snakes protect themselves by playing dead.

# What Do Snakes Eat?

    All snakes eat animals. Some eat their **prey** after they have killed it, and some eat their prey when it is alive. Snakes have a jaw that can open wide, so they can swallow their prey whole.

Large snakes eat bigger animals.
They can even eat a pig. Small snakes
eat little animals, such as worms and
grasshoppers. But most snakes will eat
anything they can catch and swallow.

Most snakes eat mice and rats. Some snakes eat only certain kinds of animals, such as lizards and frogs. Water snakes eat only fish. One African snake eats only eggs. It swallows the egg whole and then spits out its shell.

One kind of snake wraps its body around its prey. It squeezes the animal until it cannot breathe. This kind of snake is called a constrictor. It is the largest snake in the world. The anaconda is a constrictor.

Snakes do not have to eat often because they are not very active. One meal a week is enough for most snakes. Snakes can live many months without eating. Some can even wait a whole year for a meal!

# How Do Snakes Get Along with People?

Snakes can be very helpful. They help farmers by eating mice and rats that hurt crops. In some countries, such as China and Japan, people eat snake meat. Some snake venom is even used to make medicine.

Many people are afraid of snakes because they look so different from other animals. Some people think that all snakes are harmful. But they can also be helpful. They are a very important part of nature.

# Glossary

**camouflage**   coloring that helps an animal hide

**coil**   to wind into a circle

**fangs**   pointed teeth

**habitats**   places where animals live

**molting**   to shed an outer skin

**prey**   an animal eaten by another animal

**protect**   to keep from harm

**reptiles**   cold-blooded animals with backbones

**scales**   thin, flat plates that cover a reptile's body

**strike**   to hit suddenly

**venom**   poison from a snake's bite